The Amazing Fart-Man

Stinky Super Hero

J.B. O'Neil

The Amazing Fart-Man

Stinky Super Hero

Table of Contents

FREE BONUS – Amazing Fart-Man Audiobook

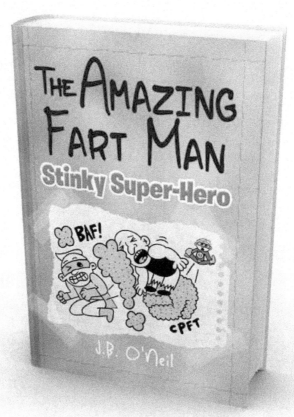

Hey gang...if you'd like to listen to the hilarious audiobook version of The Amazing Fart-Man while you follow along with this book, you can download it for free for a limited time by typing this link into your browser: http://funnyfarts.net/fartman

Enjoy!

Sweaty Summer Underpants

I woke up because the sun was coming through my window and shining right into my eyes. No alarm clocks over summer vacation! The best three months of the year!

I rolled out of bed and put on some underwear. I started to look at some pants and a shirt, but this was summer vacation—there was no room for pants and shirts here. This was the time where underwear ruled the wardrobe.

I walked downstairs to the couch and turned the television onto my favorite show, "The Wonderful World of Farts." It was a documentary series that followed farts across the world. Different people, different animals, and sometimes even plants.

There was one bad thing about the summer though—it was so hot! I was already sweating through my underpants and I had seen this episode before. I decided that I should call up my friend Stinky. He was always the best to hang out with. Besides, I just remodeled my tree house and I had a surprise for him that I knew he would love.

The Amazing Fart-Man and Stinky

A couple minutes later the doorbell rang and I answered and there was Stinky. He came inside.

"I love this show!" he said, pointing at the television.

"Hey Stinky, you gotta come to my tree house, I made some changes to it that I think you're going to like." I said. He smiled. We walked outside into my backyard.

"Stinky, I've brought you here today not just to hang out, but because you have something that makes you special. I think together we can do something amazing." Stinky looked confused.

"Stinky, you can fart like no other kid I know. Your fart prowess is second only to me. You have unlimited fart potential. You have the stinkiest farts I've ever smelled and I'm pretty sure you could fart forever if you really wanted to. Your farts are so bad that people just call you stinky now. I want you to be my sidekick." I said.

Stinky still looked confused.

"Sidekick?" He asked. "I don't know what you mean. Also, thank you. I do have great farts." We both laughed.

I looked at him and said, "I want you to be my sidekick in our superhero duo. I will be the Amazing Fart-Man and you can be my sidekick Stinky. We will fight crime and save people and we will do it by farting!"

Stinky smiled and said, "Oh yeah! We're going to be superheroes! You're going to have to teach me how to master my gas though." "Oh, I will." I said. "I will."

The Hideout

We both walked outside together and to the tree house.

"Please Stinky, you go first." I said, gesturing with my hands. I pointed to the rope ladder that lead up to the top. Stinky started to climb up the ladder, but rope ladders are hard to climb, so he was having some serious trouble.

"You can do it!" I said. He got up about three rungs and fell on his butt. I thought he sighed, but the sigh came out of the wrong end... Then I realized how bad that backwards sigh smelled. I definitely chose right with my sidekick. This kid could fart.

"Wowee, that fart almost knocked my socks off! Here, get on my back." I helped him up to his feet and he got on my back. I focused for a second and farted so hard that I looked like a spaceship taking off. The fart rocketed out of me so hard that the cloud started scorching the grass around us. We took off slowly at first, but then before we knew it we were rocketing up towards the tree house. We landed and Stinky got off.

"Wow! That was the best fart I've ever seen!" said Stinky.

"Stinky, my friend, I'll teach you everything I know."

Fart School In Session

"Stinky, with the farts that you have, you can fart anything you want. You just have to focus and picture what you want to do and let your butt do the rest."

Stinky thought about it for a second then scrunched up his face in concentration. He farted out a big green boxing glove that floated around his hand.

"That's great!" I said, "But check this out." Then I focused and started to fart. I farted out the Mona Lisa. Then I hung it on the wall.

"It looks good in green." Stinky said. Then he farted out a little dog that did a back flip before it poofed away into a regular old fart cloud. I farted out a copy of myself and we high fived before he faded away as a green mist.

"You know what Stinky, I think you've got the hang of this. I think we're ready to fight some crime." Stinky and I high-fived and got ready.

Super Hero Super-Costumes

We turned around and walked over to the computer. The screen was as big as the wall and the keyboard had about a million buttons and even more flashing lights. I walked over to the computer and I sat down in my chair and turned away from Stinky.

A bunch of robotic arms came down for a while, and then when I turned back to stinky I was wearing my superhero outfit.

"Want one of these Stinky?" I asked.

"Milo, I think you know I do."

I looked at the giant computer screen and said, "Computer, my friend here needs an extra fart proof superhero suit."

"Of course Milo. I mean Fart-Man," responded the Computer. Then, before Stinky knew what was happening he was covered up in his brand new fart proof suit and ready to fight some crime.

"Looking good Stinky."

The Fartmobile

"Computer, can you please scan the area for local crime that is happening?" I asked.

"Of course Master Fart-Man. Scanning in progress." The computer replied.

"I have found a local bully harassing a child four blocks from here. The child appears to be in some distress and is in need of assistance."

I looked at Stinky.

"Sounds perfect. Let's go save a day."

We both ran to the slide that got us out of the tree house. We slid down and flew out of the tree house. On our way down we both started farting together. We both landed in the Fart-Mobile that we had made while farting.

"Set engines to maximum." I said. We both leaned forward in our seats and farted as hard as we could. The fart rockets blasted forward and we went forward so fast that the wind started pushing out faces back.

"It's a good thing this suit is fart-proof!" screamed Stinky. "If it wasn't we'd have a real problem here." With giant green fart trails following us, we were off to save the day.

Smells Like Trouble

We screeched to a halt in front of a group of bullies, not just one. We jumped out of the Fart-Mobile and it disappeared. There were five bullies and only two of us, but we were heroes and it was our duty to stand up to overwhelming forces. Stinky and I looked at each other, a little bit worried, and then we got ready.

There were five bullies and they were all huge and covered with zits. They must have been teenagers because one of them almost had a mustache. They were surrounding the poor kid that they were bullying, pushing him around and saying mean things to him.

"Hey bullies! Stop pushing him around, or you'll have to answer to us, Fart-Man and Stinky! And trust me, you don't want to smell what we're cooking over here." I yelled.

Fart-Man and Stinky's First Fight

One of the bullies walked over to me and said, "What's that kid? You wanna try and stop me? Ha! You're just a stupid twerp." And he pushed me over. I almost fell over, but I caught myself by farting hard enough to bounce back onto my feet.

"You just made a big mistake buddy." I said. Then I jumped up into his face and farted so hard that he went flying through the air away from me. Just as he was about to hit a wall, a giant fart hand came out of Stinky's butt and caught him. The fart hand put down the bully very gently. Just as the bully was beginning to look relieved, the fart hand stuck a giant finger into the bully's nose and started picking. The bully's nose started smoking because all the nose hair burned out, and then he fainted.

"I'm not sure if the green stuff coming out is my farts or his boogers. Either way, I'm glad I'm not him right now." Said Stinky making a thumbs-up sign with his giant floating fart hand.

Bullytron!

"So I guess someone's a Mr. Tough-Guy huh?"
One of the bullies said. Then they all huddled
together and started climbing onto one another.
Stinky and I looked at each other confused. We
had never seen anything like what they were
doing before. After a moment the bully pile
began to rise up into the air. When it finished,
all of the bullies had joined together and created
a giant super bully. Each of the limbs was a bully
acting as a part of the new giant bully.

"We are Bullytron, we are invincible!" Bullytron
shouted.

Well, even if they had made a giant bully, there was no way that I was about to stop being a superhero, so I stepped between the giant super bully and its victim. Nobody was about to get past me.

A Stinky Plan

I looked over at Stinky and nodded to him, then he nodded back at me. We both knew what we had to do to save the day. Stinky ran forward and jumped into the air. While he was up there he farted out a skateboard and landed on it. Then he farted it up into the air and started to fly around the top of the super bully. He flew faster and faster around and around the super bully.

Bullytron tried to spin fast enough to watch him the whole time, but Stinky was flying too fast for it to keep up with. The super bully soon got so dizzy that it could hardly stand. That's when we knew we had our chance. Stinky flew towards me and picked me up, and then he flew straight up into the sky, as high as he could.

"Now!" I yelled, and he dropped me right on top of the super bully, who was still having trouble standing. I went flying through the air straight for it.

Bullytron's Butts Are Kicked

As I flew towards Bullytron I farted out a fist that went flying ahead of me. It flew at the bullies and slammed into the bully who was acting as the head. Immediately, Bullytron launched a counter-attack with a bully-punch.

A whole bully was flying up at me. It was going to hit me. There was nothing that I could do about it.

Right before the bully arm hit me a giant green fart shield appeared before me and stopped the first in its tracks. The shield flew right back into where it came from—Stinky's butt! It flew back into Stinky's butt and then came out of his other end as a re-farted burp. The terrible cloud drifted over Bullytron and knocked it out cold. All of the bullies fell apart, back into individuals. They all fell into a big bully pile, covered in the fart burp.

"Hahaha. Well, done boys. To be honest, I thought you would have more trouble with Bullytron than that." Said a mysterious voice. Stinky and I turned around to see an equally mysterious man, wearing a long cloak and a deep hood.

The Cheese Cutter

"Hello there." He said, waving at us. "I had heard a rumor of a new crime fighting duo in this city, but I had no idea that they were quite so gifted as the two of you boys. If I didn't start my evil plan now, you two could really become a thorn in my side."

He continued to walk towards us.

"Who are you?" I demanded. I make it a habit to not trust guys with hoods who greet me by creepily laughing.

"Who? Me?" He asked. "I'm just a man with a vision, and that vision happens to not include

31

the either of you. So," He pulled out a giant red pulsing button. "I would prefer that you both put an end to this whole superhero thing." He shrugged and continued to approach us.

"You can call me the Cheese Cutter."

The Kidnapping

"I suppose you're wondering what my big plan is boys. Well, I'll tell you because I know that there is no way that you can stop me. The first part is to take this small child." He pointed at the kid who was being bullied. Then he hit the giant red button that he was holding. A huge net flew out of nowhere and a group of men dressed in black and flying with jet packs flew in from out of nowhere. They picked up the kid in the net and started to fly away.

Stinky and I farted ourselves into the air chasing after the men with jet packs, but they were so fast we couldn't keep up. We both started desperately weaving our farts together to make an even bigger fart net, which we threw over them.

It was a good idea, but we might have made the fart net a little bit too big, because all the men flew right through it. They got away completely.

Cheese Cutter's Threat

We tried to follow them, but jet packs go way faster than farts so we had to give up the chase. By the time Stinky and I landed, the Cheese Cutter was gone. We looked around everywhere, but there was nothing left. We just stood there, wondering what our next step was when a piece of paper flew into Stinky's face and stuck to him. He fell over, clawing at his face trying to get it off. When he did, he looked at it, and then looked at me. He was frowning.

He handed me the piece of paper. It was a note from the Cheese Cutter that said, "If you ever want to see this poor child again, you will give up this dream of being a superhero, but more

than anything you have to give up farting.
Forever!"

Give up farting!? I could never do that!

The End of Fart-Man!?

I had no idea what to do. I was a superhero. I had super fart powers. It was my destiny, my responsibility, my life. What was the Amazing Fart-Man without farts? The Amazing Man? Ridiculous!

Stinky looked at me and said, "Well, there's no way you can give up crime fighting, or farting. You're a hero! What will kids in need do when they're getting bullied? Who will come and help them?"

He was pleading me to keep helping those in need.

"I know Stinky, but I don't think that I can risk the safety of an innocent kid. I cannot risk the safety of kids who I'm supposed to be protecting. That's the opposite of being a superhero! I'm here to protect, not to put in harm's way. I think that I'm going to have to stop." I said. I started to walk home, defeated. I was so lost. I had no idea what to do anymore.

The Answer

I got back to my tree house and looked up at it, then climbed the ladder in. I opened up the bottom hatch that lead in and walked over to my chair. I sat down in it and took my mask off and stared at it.

"What should I do?" I asked the mask, but I was really asking myself.

"What do I do!?" I shook the mask. I heard a fart and Stinky came flying up through the window to land next to me. He focused for a second then farted. It was a ripe one. Then the words floated in front of me.

"What are you going to do now?"

It's not often that you get to smell a question that someone has asked you. I had no idea what the answer was, but I did know it was the most disgusting one that I had ever smelled. I waved my hand through it and made it disappear.

The Return of Fart-Man and Stinky!

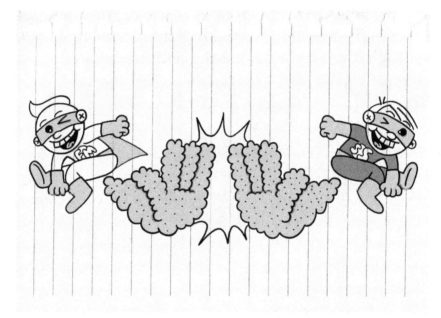

I stayed sitting in the chair, still thinking about the kid who got kidnapped because of me.

"Fart-Man, this is your duty! You have to put the mask back on and go get that kid! We can do it together! You taught me everything I know." Stinky said.

I started to think he was right. If I didn't go save the kid, then who would? My fart powers got the kid into this whole mess, so now it was my fart powers that were going to have to get him out. The Cheese Cutter was a villain anyway. There's no way that he would let that kid go even if I did what he asked. That's what bad guys do. They lie, especially when it's just mean to do it.

I looked up at Stinky and smiled.

"Stinky...I can't do it alone." I said. I put my mask back on and stood up. Stinky and I jumped into the air and farted out giant green hands and high-fived so hard that the hands exploded.

Chasing the Cheese-Cutter

"Stinky, I couldn't have done this without you. You're the best sidekick that a Fart-Man could ask for. You showed me the light and now we're going to follow it!" I said to Stinky. He smiled back at me.

"That's why I think that we should be known as the crime fighting duo, the Fartners! The unstoppable fart team!" We jumped back into the Fart-Mobile.

"Where do you think the Cheese Cutter's evil lair is Fart-Man?" asked Stinky. We drove around looking for it.

"Well," I said, "there is that giant creepy building in the middle of town that has the huge brick of cheese with the even bigger knife going through it. I guess we could start looking for him there." And away we rocketed in our Fart-Mobile.

The Note-So-Secret Lair

We pulled up in front of the giant building in the middle of town and got out. There was a sign out front that said, "Cheese Cutter's secret evil lair. No loitering."

"Well, I guess this is the place." I said. Stinky and I looked at each other and walked towards the door.

"We might have to think of a plan to get in. He'll have some good security." Stinky said. I walked up and opened the door.

Stinky shrugged.

"Or the door is unlocked and we can walk right in."

So we opened the front door and walked in. There was a thick green fart trail that started at the door and lead up a giant spiral staircase.

"Think we should follow that?" I asked.

"Well, considering the security at the door, this probably leads straight to his office." Said Stinky. We both laughed.

Evil Genius Death Trap #313

We followed the fart trail all the way up to the top of the building to a door that said "Cheese Cutter's secret office. No soliciting."

We looked at each other.

"I can't believe that worked." I said.

We opened the door.

Inside was an enormous office with a desk sitting at the other end. Behind the desk was Cheese Cutter, with his hands folded together, staring at us. Hanging above him was a cage holding the kid that Cheese Cutter took before.

Between us and him was what looked like an army of teenagers. Half of them almost had mustaches and the other half had more of their faces covered in pimples than without pimples.

Cheese Cutter spun around in his chair once, and then he snapped his fingers. The cage started moving towards the open window and the army of teenagers attacked us. They flew through the air like a swarm of angry wasps.

At Least 2 Bullies

The fight had begun. Stinky and I went running forward, trying to get to the kid in the cage before it made its way to the window, then out of the window, but that was not going to be easy.

I jumped up and put my hands under my butt and farted out two giant green fart hands. They covered my regular hands. I ran at the bad guys trying to punch my way through them. When I hit a bully in the face, their nose would start to smoke and they'd fall over, unconscious from the smell.

While I was busy knocking out bullies, Stinky ran to the other side of the room and farted a snowplow onto his head. Then he took a few warm-up steps like a bull does before he charges and farted himself forward. After he built up enough speed, he went flying through whole groups of bullies, knocking them over like bowling balls.

Before we knew it there were bullies flying everywhere and there were piles of them on the ground, passed out. No matter how many fell though, it seemed like there were always about a hundred more ready to go. I couldn't understand how this many bullies could even fit in a room.

Caught!

More and more bullies fell, but no matter how many we took down, there were always more between us and the kid who kept moving closer and closer to the open window. The fart cloud in the room started to get so thick that we were all having a little trouble breathing.

Man these farts were bad.

I kept trying to move forward, but my eyes were starting to water from the all of the terrible farts. I couldn't quite see straight anymore and that's when it happened; one of the bullies landed on me. Then another and another. I tried to fart my way out, but there were so many bullies on me that the gas couldn't escape.

The cage was only a few feet from the open window now.

Cheese Cutter stood up from his chair and began to slowly walk towards me. I couldn't see Stinky anymore, but I could hear muffled farts coming from behind me. I guess he was buried in bullies too. Cheese Cutter stood over me laughing.

"Well, well, well. What do we have here? The Amazing Fart-Manman come to save the day? How's that working out for you? I thought I told you that if you continued this superhero lifestyle, you would never see your friend here again."

Cheese Cutter's Evil (Smelling) Plan

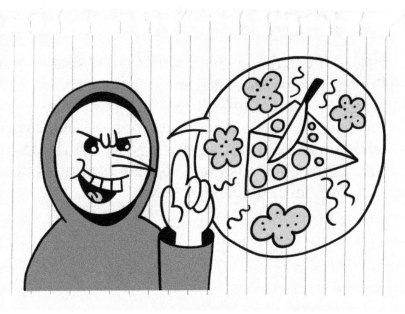

"You'll never get away with this!" I yelled at him from under about a hundred bullies.

"Get away with what? You don't even know what my plan is." He said.

"I plan to remove all of the superheroes from the world so that there is nobody to get in my way for when I try to take over the world. It's just easier that way. My plan, young hero, is to construct the world's largest brick of cheese, then cut it! I will fill the world with the worst fart smell that anybody has ever smelled! Then, when the world is full of fart smell, everyone will forget what actual farts smell like, then nobody will ever be able to enjoy them ever again! Nobody will even smell the farts over the cheese. Once that has happened, without the joy of farts, the world will fall into despair and offer me no resistance as I conquer them!" Cheese Cutter was starting to get pretty excited now.

"Even if you do get away with this," I said, "even if your plan works and you defeat me today, someday, someone will rise up against you because that's what goodness does. Goodness rises up against evil, just as a good fart rises up from the couch cushion! You can beat me, but you can never defeat goodness."

Super Farts Save the Day!

That just made Cheese Cutter laugh. He started to laugh so hard that he farted. He continued to laugh even as he pulled another ominous red button from under his cloak. He held it up in front of my face and pushed it. The bottom of the cage opened up and dropped the kid out the window.

"No!" I yelled. I focused all the remaining strength within me, and farted so hard that the pile of bullies all flew off of me and smashed through the walls, leaving bully-shaped holes behind them. The fart came out with such force that a mushroom cloud formed and the floor beneath me was completely burnt away.

I flew towards the window so fast that my eyelids started peeling back. I chased the falling kid through the air and caught him. I farted out a fart-parachute that we both hung from, butts up. Then I started farting into my fart parachute and we went back up to the top floor.

The Big Cheese Is Cut Forever

I floated back in the window and dropped the kid off safely.

"Thanks, Fart-Man!" he said, pinching his nose shut. Then I looked at Stinky, and we both knew what to do. We combined our powers and farted chains and locks at Cheese Cutter, which locked him to the floor and the wall. He wasn't laughing anymore.

"It looks like good rose up a little bit sooner than you were expecting." I said to him. He started begging for mercy and pleaded with me to let him go.

"Stinky, I think the jail has a room reserved for Mr. Cheese Cutter." I said. Stinky nodded. We both pointed our butts at Cheese Cutter and farted. The farts all wove together and wrapped around him. The bullies who could still move looked up and watched as the farts combined to make two beautiful angelic wings, except they were green and smelled terrible. The wings flapped and flapped and before long Cheese Cutter was flying out the window and into jail.

Stinky and I walked back to my tree house, put on our regular old clothes and started planning out our next big summer vacation adventure. The world was safe...for now.

More Books by J.B. O'Neil

Hi Gang! I hope you liked "The Amazing Fart-Man." Here are some more funny, cool books I've written that I think you'll like too...

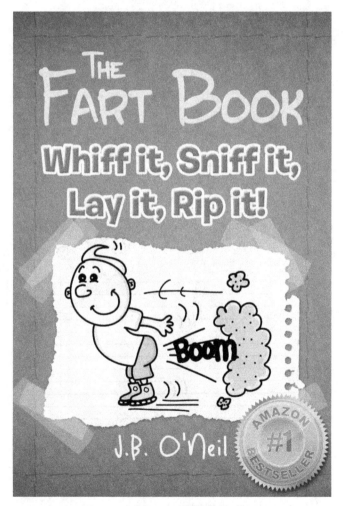

http://jjsnip.com/fart-book

And...

http://jjsnip.com/booger-fart-books

Silent but Deadly...As a Ninja Should Be!

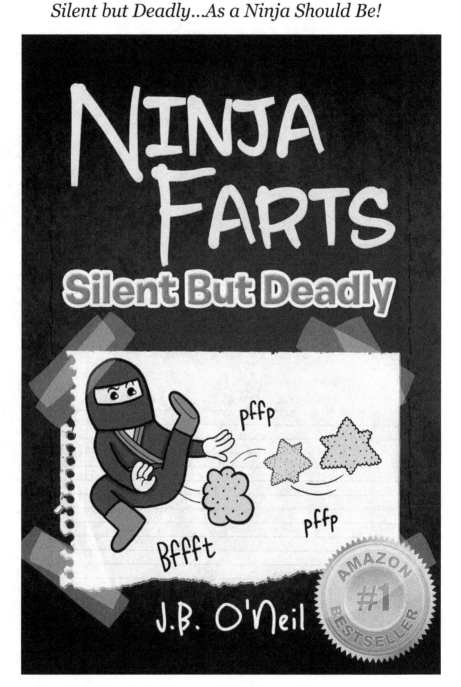

http://jjsnip.com/ninja-farts-book

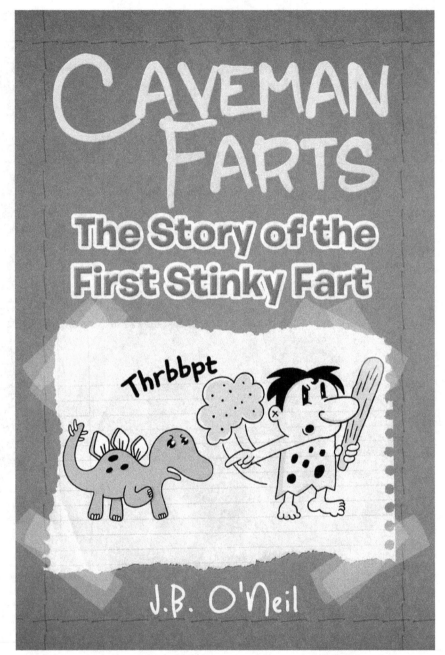

http://jjsnip.com/caveman-farts

Think twice before you blame the dog!

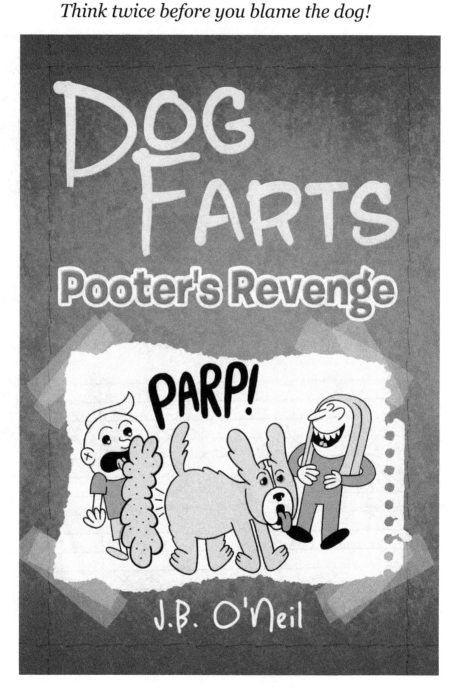

A long time ago, in a galaxy fart, fart away...

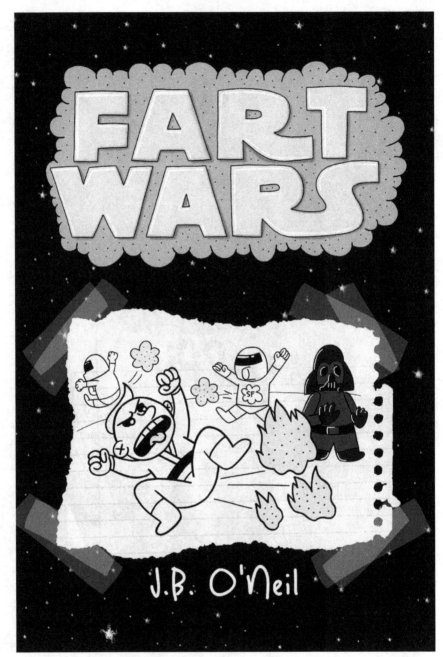

http://jjsnip.com/fart-wars

We are the Farts! The Mighty Fighting Farts!

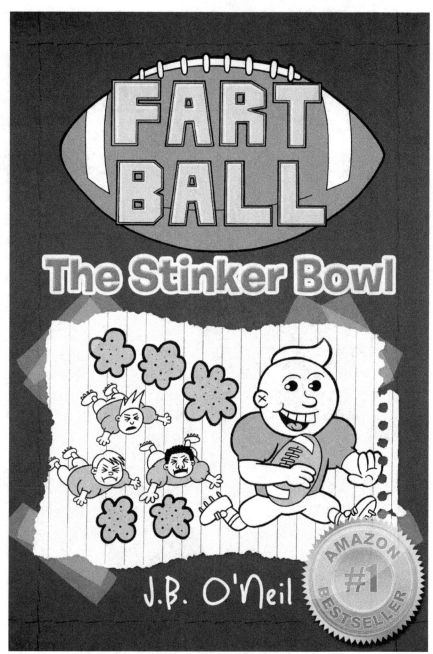

http://jjsnip.com/fartball

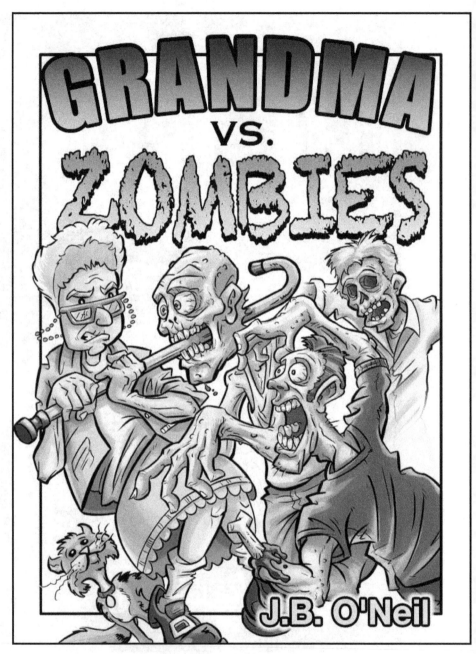

http://jjsnip.com/gvz

CPSIA information can be obtained
at www.ICGtesting.com
Printed in the USA
LVHW030258120320
649742LV00011B/1113

9 781492 220312